MEMORIES AND REFLECTIONS

THE COLLECTED POEMS OF ALLAN G. MATTHEWS
(1910 – 1977)

Order this book online at www.trafford.com
or email orders@trafford.com

Most Trafford titles are also available at major online book retailers.

Edited by James Fontana.

Note for Librarians: A cataloguing record for this book is available from Library and Archives Canada at www.collectionscanada.ca/amicus/index-e.html

Printed in Victoria, BC, Canada.

ISBN: 978-1-4251-8929-7 (Soft)

We at Trafford believe that it is the responsibility of us all, as both individuals and corporations, to make choices that are environmentally and socially sound. You, in turn, are supporting this responsible conduct each time you purchase a Trafford book, or make use of our publishing services. To find out how you are helping, please visit www.trafford.com/responsiblepublishing.html

Our mission is to efficiently provide the world's finest, most comprehensive book publishing service, enabling every author to experience success. To find out how to publish your book, your way, and have it available worldwide, visit us online at www.trafford.com

Rev. date 8/14/2009

www.trafford.com

North America & International
toll-free: 1 888 232 4444 (USA & Canada)
phone: 250 383 6864 ♦ fax: 812 355 4082
email: info@trafford.com

TABLE OF CONTENTS

ALLAN GEORGE MATTHEWS
biographical note

ALLAN GEORGE MATTHEWS, our father, was born one of five children, three boys and two girls, on the 26th of October, 1910, in Taynuilt, Argyllshire in the Scottish Highlands. His father, our grandfather, George William Matthews, was a stonemason. At the time, this was a fortuitous calling for any Scot seeking to emigrate to Canada because construction of the neo-Gothic buildings which were to make up Parliament Hill in Ottawa was still very much in progress.

So, in 1929 at the age of nineteen, Allan Matthews and his father left Taynuilt to come to Ottawa. His father had secured employment working the stone for the Confederation Building that was to compliment the Centre Block of Parliament Hill.

They already had a contact in the Ottawa area. Archibald Campbell, who was grand-dad's brother-in-law and dad's uncle, owned and operated the Campbell Sandstone Quarries in Bell's Corners, a town very much outside the city of Ottawa in those days. Archibald Campbell had been instrumental in "bringing out" granddad and our father to work here.

The arrangement attracting our granddad and father was one that was common enough in those days. They would work in Canada for two years, accumulate their savings, then return to Scotland.

But the great depression changed everything.

Instead of returning to Scotland, George brought the rest of the family here. That necessary migration of the balance of the Matthews family to Canada, a wise and ultimately successful move, never the less reduced Dad to tears.

Time passed. They all worked and prospered. Then Allan met the lady who was to secure his destiny forever in Canada. Lillian Emily May Iles was her name. Our mother! They eloped and were married in 1936 at the Church of the Good Shepherd in Wakefield, Quebec. The church still stands there today.

But that was not the only proposal that, once accepted, was to forever confirm Allan's life in Canada.

In those days soccer was a favourite pass-time, particularly among the immigrants who had imported the game into Canada from Europe. Competition was vigorous among the many companies and businesses that fielded teams in the Ottawa league. And Allan, it seems, had developed into a skillful and formidable player. Now in his mid-twenties, he was probably at the top of his game and physical conditioning when he was approached with a tempting offer: If he would agree to play for the E. B. Eddy Co. soccer team there would be permanent employment for him with the company in its Hull paper mill.

He accepted. And certainly the job was permanent because he spent his entire working career with E. B. Eddy until he retired in the late seventies. Ultimately he played for Ottawa United ("The Scottish") and was mentioned in sports news dispatches out of Toronto, Chicago and Ottawa, particularly with regard to his participation in the Inter-Service Soccer League.

Could it have been the birth of twin sons that brought out a hidden talent in Allan, about that time? Glenn and I were born on the 18th of November, 1939 and from that time forward, until 1953-54, dad wrote poetry and songs.

A news clipping from the period describes dad, during his breaks from the heat and noise of the paper machines, reaching for a pencil stub and scrap of paper to begin working on a new poem. The inspiration was centered around memories of Scotland, the heroics and horrors of war, the love of family and his new country. Most of the poems contained here were published in either the Ottawa Journal or the Ottawa Evening Citizen.

Dad also submitted his poetry and song lyrics to several publishers both in Canada and the United States. Some were used, some not. Most however resulted in a reply from the publishers complimenting his work. He also produced articles for various magazines- -The McNab Historical Association, The Anthology of American Humor, and the Pulp and Paper Magazine of Canada (which invited him to produce more works for them, including a series "Timber Tales". Three articles were published in the local press (it is impossible to say which newspapers): the Weird Tale of Headless Valley in the Yukon and Northwest Territories, Logging In Olden Times, and Ottawa Clicked First Aerial Shutter, on the birth of aerial photography.

In an article, published by the Bell Syndicate, "Nepean

Sandstone Used for Parliament Buildings", dad described the source and methods used for finding the stone that would become the Peace Tower and Parliament Buildings. He explained why Aberdeen was called the Granite City, why Kingston should be the Limestone City and why Ottawa will be known as the Sandstone City.

Dad's writing seemed to come to and end when Glenn and I started playing the bagpipes with the Cameron Highlanders of Ottawa. His enthusiasm for our endeavors seemed to turn him from writing poetry to concentrate on making sure Glenn and I and our friends made it to practice and to parades.

After retiring dad took a job at Parkdale United Church to fill his time and supplement his income.

Dad loved Canada yet his longing for Scotland never diminished. But he always said that by the time he could do it, it was too late. Too much in Scotland would have changed. There would be no sentimental journey back to Taynuilt.

He died on the 11th of September, 1977.

By way of postscript we would like to say that in the basements and attics of homes across this country there no doubt are many stories and poems lying unread and unpublished. Thanks to the involvement, persistence and guidance of one individual, Mr. Justice James Fontana, this tiny part of Canadian history will not be lost.

Garry and Glenn Matthews
September 16, 2008

COMPILER'S NOTE

MORE THAN FIFTEEN YEARS AGO Garry Matthews first handed me the thick sheaf of papers that were his father's collected poems. After reading them several times they seemed to take on greater and greater significance. When Garry invited me to 'do something' with them, with a view to getting them into book form, I was complimented.

It is my view—the view of a non-poet, by the way—that the body of work, taken as a whole, provides an ever-deepening insight into the poet's journey through life, the journey of the Scottish immigrant to Canada who ultimately surrenders to the call of his new country. It is a fascinating journey.

Taken individually the reader may find, in some of the poems, a hint of Yeats, in others the cadence of Kipling. The soul of the lyrical poet is evident in all of them.

The poems are presented exactly as Allan George Matthews wrote them.

They have not been altered in any way. The phrasing is the same. There has been no tampering with Matthews' punctuation. Sometimes the poet capitalized the first letter of certain words, in the middle of a phrase or sentence, for his own effect. These have not been changed. In one or two of the poems there are blank spaces where a word has been omitted. This was either because the poet left it blank while he waited for an inspired word to present itself, (which it never did) or because the word could not be ascertained in the old, faded penciled manuscript.

Some very minor formatting and amending of obvious typographical irregularities were the only changes.

James Fontana.
Ottawa, Ontario. September 16, 2008

DOWN MEMORY LANE

I often go back to old Scotland,
In my journeys down memory lane.
Back to the land of the heather,
In fancy I wander again.
I climb the peaks of Ben Burnish,
So craggy and weathered by time.
Smelling the scent of the heather,
Mingled wi' that o' the pine.
I tread along paths well remembered,
From childhoods adventurous days.
Scenes from these far time recalling,
As I follow their meandering ways.
Though its been long since I left there,
I vision it all once again.
When I go back to old Scotland
In my journeys down memory lane.

Notes

A TOAST TAE OUR RABBIE

A toast tae our Rabbie, tae Rabbie a toast
Auld Scotia's pride an' auld Scotia's boast.
An' thought it's been lang, since our
Rabbie has died,
An' other poets lived an' other poets tried
Tae better his work, their efforts were sma'
Our Rabbie by far's still the best o' them a'.
He sang of auld Scotland, o' mountain an' glen,
O' castle an' cottage, an' wee "but an' ben."
The mist on the heather, the dew on the grass,
The dreams o' a lad, in the kiss o' a lass.
And tae us who wandered sae far frae our Name,
Tae obscurity maybe – an' some to reach fame,
In lang lonely moments we go back again,
Borne on the magic that flowed frae his pen.
A toast then, to Rabbie, tae Rabbie toast,
Auld Scotia's pride, an' auld Scotia's boast,
Like the thistle, our Rab is o' Scotland a part,
An' his name lives forever, enshrined in each heart.

Notes

DEEP IN MY HEART

Deep in my heart
I hear the pipes play.
Come back again it seems that they say.
Back to your homeland back to the glen
And walk thru' the brave purple heather again.

Notes

HIGHLANDER'S LAMENT

I'm wearyin' for Scotland and the sight o' heather hills,
The glory of her mountains and the music of her rills.
I'm wearyin' for Scotland and the bracken on the brae.
And to stroll again the gloamin' at the ending of the day.
I'm wearyin' for Scotland, for each corrie and each
knowe,
To see the mist at dawning as it wreaths
Ben Lomonds brow.
And the new-born sun, long-fingered,
chasing shadows from the glen,
And the smoke ascending lightly from each
wee bit "but an' ben".
I'm wearyin' for Scotland and the sight o' Heather hills,
For the glory of her mountains and the music of her rills.
Just the thought o' purple heather,
and o' mountains rising high,
Will start the mind to dreaming –
and the heart to give a sigh.

Notes

A BROKEN DREAM

Hitler he did meditate
And then he handed out the bait.
Benito, he did calculate
And thought, Why shouldn't I be great?
Together then they set a date
To England they would penetrate.
They had a binge to celebrate
And England they professed to hate.
Goeble's was there, just so sedate
And Goering quite emalculate
The papers they did circulate
That England was to meet her fate
Said Hitler, "You will get this straight.
We must do this before too late."
The English we will educate
Their social standing elevate
We'll travel at an awful rate
In three weeks, I will lordly gait
Shall stroll the Strand and fascinate
The people into such a state
Their hearts I'm sure to captivate.
Alas for Adolph's lovely dream
It wandered slightly off the beam.

He's far from being world supreme
And from his troops he's lost the cream.
Benny too, it' plainly seen
Doth mourn for what life what might have been.
But some day coming soon I guess
They'll get a plane in Inverness
And to some sturdy Scot confess
They want to board with Rudolph Hess.

A HOME IN THE MOON?

*(Based on a recent news report that a trip to the moon,
in the very near future, will only require five days.)*

We're living in the dawning
Of a new and different age.
Soon chasing off to outer space,
Will be the current rage.
It really sounds quite interesting,
That coming some day soon,
Each of us can pack a grip
And travel to the moon.
When tired out with toiling,
At the ending of the day,
We can spend a quiet evening
As we tour the Milky Way.
The mystery of Orian's Belt,
The Sisters and the Dipper,
Now soon will be quite commonplace,
Ignored by every tripper.
And then, perhaps, my search will end,
And I will live contented,
For maybe on the moon I'll find
A house that isn't rented.
For I have searched this planet, Earth,
Till gloom, my heart, has clouded,
And my decision is, you bet,
The darn thing's overcrowded.

Notes

A LETTER FROM BENITO

I've just had a letter from Benny,
The jolly old braggart of Rome;
He tells me he's spending the summer,
Camped in the cellar at home.
He tells me: indeed he seems worried;
He finds it tough standing the gaff
Since his legions in Libya, remember?
Were halted and scattered like chaff.
He claims he is being neglected;
His business, we know, has been slack.
There isn't a country remaining
That he can stab in the back.

On page three he mentions his navy;
In fancy I hear him sigh
As he uses a half-page explaining
The reason his sailors are shy.
In the letter he says they're allergic
To battle, its smoke and its noise.
But assures me that they were in peace time
The bravest and boldest of boys
He doesn't sound too optimistic
But writes with a most injured air
Of the troubles besetting friend Adolf

In his fight with the big Russian Bear.
The letter was really pathetic;
Peace now, he says, is his hope.
I guess he can see that the Axis
Are nearing the end of their rope.
He didn't say what his address is,
So I'm sorry I can't answer back
And have it delivered by air mail
Tied to a bomb on a rack.

ADVICE TO THE YOUNG

Cherish the days of your youth, lad,
Store up these memories so gay.
They'll warm you when you get old, lad,
And the sunshine of youth's gone away.
Then your thoughts will drift down the
trail, lad, And over again you'll enjoy,
The pleasure filled days that you
knew, lad, In the carefree life of a boy.

Notes

ARMCHAIR I KAVELLER

Often I've heard of the beauties of Erin,
And tho' never destined these beauties to see,
In fancy I've wandered the dells of Killarney,
And shamrocks I've picked in the vale of Tralee.
The mountains of Mourne I've seen in their glory,
And wandered the summit where lonely winds sigh
While down in the valleys each lake, clear and placid,
Reflect back the blue of the soft summer sky.
The son of the Shannon I've heard in its flowing,
And gay and light-hearted it sounded to me.
As twisting and turning by town and by hamlet
Gaily it followed its course to the sea.
Kilkenny, Portrush and the Glens of Antrim,
Donegal, County Down and Kildare.
In vision I know, as to Erin I go,
From the depth of my old rocking-chair.

Notes

ATOMIC AFFECTION

This jolly old world with the peace-flag unfurled,
Has a future that's broad and elastic.
Where an act of aggression will bring a tough session
Of measures both fearsome and drastic.
It's outlawed, no dice, to carve out a slice
Of a country that's smaller or weaker.
A splendid condition that curbs the ambition
Of guys who would crawl up and sneak 'er.
According to plan, now the footsteps of man,
Are treading the highway together.
The "big shots," the masses, the folks of all classes
Are really just birds of a feather.
It's found, yes indeed, that each race and each creed
Have affection for each that is comic.
All hate now has shifted, and man has been gifted,
With love that is surely atomic.

Notes

BACK ON THE JOB

Exchanging my gun for an oil-can
Was something I did with a will.
It's alright to roam but it's swell to be home,
Back on my job in the mill.
I'm glad that the task is all over
And the Axis again in their place.
With the peace flag unfurled Again o'er the world,
All the horrors of war to erase.
Exchanging my khaki for civvies
Was something that gave me a thrill.
Now the smell of hot gears Is the worst of my fears,
Back on my job in the mill.

Notes

CALL OF THE WOODS

"By gee, by gosh," said ol' Batiste,
"I love be lumberjack.
And when the winter time she come ,
Always Batiste go back.
For when de snow is on the groun'
De air so crisp an' fine,
Batiste he see the great nort' woods
Where grow the spruce an' pine.
Dey seem to call to ol' Batiste,
Come back, my fren', come back.
Dat's why, for forty year an' more,
Batiste been lumberjack."

Notes

CAN WE BE FRIENDS FOR A' THAT

(With the usual apologies for an act of piracy)

Then let us pray that come it may,
As come it will for a' that,
That sense and worth, o' er a' the earth,
may bear the gree and a' that;
For a' that, and a' that,
It's coming yet for a' that,
That man to man the wary o'er,
Shall brithers be for a' that.
-Burns.
But lost, it's taking quite a while,
Folks won't agree and a' that,
They scowl at us instead o' smile,
And talk of war and a' that.
For a' that and a' that,
Their talk of might and a' that,
We still extend the friendly hand,
And pity them for a' that.
You see yon birkies in Berlin,
Wi' struttin' walk and a' that,
They're ripe for trouble, sure as sin,
But only fools for a' that.
For a' that, and a' that,
Their tommy-guns and a' that,

Ye canna yoke up honest folk,
As they'll find out for a' that.
But still we hope that we can cope,
Wi' threats of might and a' that,
And if we give them so much rope,
They'll hang themselves for a' that,
For a' that, and a' that,
Their guns and tanks and a' that,
The cause of right shall win the fight,
And triumph still for a' that.

CHRISTMAS WISH

Anticipation lights each eye,
As rapidly the hours fly,
Bringing quickly on the way
The joy and mirth of Christmas Day.
Each little girl, each little boy,
Is dreaming of some fancied toy
That near their stocking will be found
When Santa Claus completes his round.
I only wish that I were young,
And once again my stocking hung
Beside the fireside's rosy glow,
As it did so long ago.
No use, for those old days, to sigh,
Santa now just passes by,
And tho' his virtues still sing,
The things I want he cannot bring.

Notes

CONSCIENCE

I see it standing bleak and grey,
Each evening at the close of day.
A ruined castle `mid the trees,
That brings back fearful memories.
I see in vision bright and clear,
A spurred and booted cavalier,
And in his arms a lady fair,
Of wondrous shape and lustrous hair.
I shudder for again 'tis night,
No moon, no stars, no earthly light.
And death that breedeth in the dark,
In furtive shape slips through the park.
I hold my breath and waiting seem
To hear an awful rending scream
That rises, quivering, on the air
Then disappear's I know not where.
I seem to see that shape again,
Upon whose brown the mark of Cain
Shall this night and always be
Branded for eternity.

I saw him as he raised his blade
I saw the flashing arc it made
I saw, too, his target clear,
The sweetheart of the cavalier.
I heard him as he stood and cried,
Up in that room where love had died
"I call upon the powers that be,
To witness this I've done to thee,
My love you spurned. no more you can
Share your love with mortal man!"

CONTRAST

A blackbird calls from a pine-tree limb,
A robin sings in a hollow.
And high o'erhead in darting flight
On swift wings is a swallow.
A butterfly, in wavering dance,
Alights on a nearby thicket.
While out from behind a fallen log
Comes the rasping cry of a cricket.
A grey squirrel scolds from a safe retreat
High in a leafy bower.
And a hurrying bee with a busy hum
Alights on a purple flower ...
In the changing scenes no more we see
The darting swift-winged swallow.
No blackbird calls from the pine-tree limb
And the robin's gone from the hollow.
The butterfly, the busy bee,
The rasping singing cricket
Are gone like a wistful memory,
And the leaves are brown on the thicket.

Notes

DEAR MA

This eye you see a-swelling'
Is the cause of a mistake.
I only started talkin'
Of the pies Ma used to make.
The missis got belligerent,
I really don't know why.
And this is where the rollin' pin,
Caught me in the eye.
But gosh, it got monotonous
This eatin'outa tins,
Three days last week, I `ad sardines,
I almost sprouted fins.
But I was bein' helpful You could throw me for a loop,
Jest the way that she exploded,
When I said how Ma made soup.
She then got kinda nasty,
When I mentioned just for fun,
If she could find the recipe
How Ma made current bun.
Of course I also mentioned
Jest the way that Ma made toast."
And of the way she cooked the spuds
And how she browned a roast.

But I was bein' helpful, see,
She needn't have got mad.
She missed me with the fryin' pan
I'm glad her aim was bad.
With her I tried to reason
But she only answered 'baa'
And that is why tomorrow I'm a-goin' home to Ma.

EACH LITTLE THING

Each little thing you do for me
Makes brighter still the memory
Of minutes spent, Together
Memories that shan't grow old
But down within the heart enfold
Their deep content.

Notes

ETERNAL PEACE

Eternal peace, that is our quest.
Eternal peace, its hope and rest.
Eternal peace, our souls have cried
For that: how may men have died?
Eternal peace for that we fight.
Eternal peace which is our right.
A greater brotherhood of man
For that we fight and die and plan.
And now on every far flung front
There's gallant men who bear the brunt
Of hate, thats surely spawned in hell.
The blood and sweat, the shot and shell.
Eternal peace shall come to pass,
When on this earth man breathes his last.
When man is mingled with the dust
His guns of war forever hushed.
When his cities are mouldering heaps of stone
And to his God he has atoned.
When his dreams of might are buried deep
And his common clay's in its last long sleep.
Then the winds shall mock at his shattered towers
At the deeds he done, and his dreams of power
For the day of man must surely cease,
Ere upon this earth, there's eternal peace.

Notes

FAIRYLAND

I took a trip to fairyland
That loveliest of places,
And there I met some little men
With little elfin faces.
They were dressed in suits of green,
And wore three-cornered hats.
With funny shoes upon their feet,
And little buttoned spats.
They were all so merry
And laughed aloud with glee,
Their capers and their antics,
Were wonderful to see.
They took me up to see their king,
Who had a great long beard,
He sat upon a little throne
And looked at me quite scared.
I heard him whisper "She's so big"'
Tho' really I'm quite small,
I didn't like to tell the king,
I won't be five 'til fall.

He asked me if I'd like to stay
With them in fairyland,
And said that he could make me small
If he waved his magic wand.
I thanked the king and then I said
"I must be on my way"
But promised him that I'd come back
And visit him some day.
They led me down a leafy path,
And through a small red gate,
And said you'd better hurry,
For it's getting awful late.

FALSE ALARM

To twelve thousand students the Fuehrer was speaking,
His words flowing out like a tap that was leaking:
Flanked by his stout-hearted Reichsmarshal Goering
His words, so I hear, were not a bit boring.
He outlined the history of the great German nation
And received in reply a heiling ovation.
His chest he stuck out and his voice was a scream
When he said : "We alone in this war are supreme;
We'll soon have this big Russian bear in the bag.
" And he twirled his moustache and hollered "Der Tag."
"We have the power and I know we can fool
That man Uncle Sam and his friend Johnny Bull
Then he paused for a sound was borne on the breeze
(It wasn't Jack Benny playing the flight of the Bees)
Muted by distance, it caused him to wonder,
The sky was quite clear, so it couldn't be thunder.
And he cried, "Its an air raid, Dumkompts,
Donnerwetter,
Someone give me a hole, the deeper the better.
Where is the Marshal he'll know what is best?
And turning, found Goering, his chins on his chest.

Then the Fuehrer turned purple,
his rage over-pouring
For it wasn't an air raid
'twas just Goering snoring..
Oh, Lord stretch out thy hand and bless
All sinners such as me
Imbue their hearts with Heavenly love
For all eternity

FOR ALL ETERNITY

Oh, Lord stretch out thy hand and bless
All sinners such as me
Imbue their hearts with Heavenly love
For all eternity

Notes

"FORE"

*(Some people maintain that golf originated in Holland,
while others, well...)*

In days of old, least so I'm told,
On the heather hills of Lomond
A wee Scots lad a brainwave had
As he slept there in the gloaming'.
With his claymore slick a hick'ry stick
He cut -and then he bent it.
And most folk say that is the way
That golfing was invented.
Just like disease fanned by a breeze
There's millions now afflicted.
The young, the old, the meek, the bold,
To golf are now addicted.
Up with the lark they play till dark,
The hills and valleys roamin',
And bless the Scot who had the thought
To play there in the gloamin'.

Notes

FORTY YEARS AGO AND MORE

Forty years ago and more
I left my Scottish hame
And o'er the sea to Canada
A wee bit lad I came
Just to make a fortune
And to reach a high estate
Only to discover
I was Fifty years too late
Depression hit the country
And the going got kinda tough
You couldn't even buy a job
Just living was quite rough
And then I went to Eddys
And got a job – thru luck
The money wasn't very much
At least it was a buck.
Free from want and free from care
Free from all earthly sin
Open wide the door of love
And let such people in.

Notes

FREE

Free from want and free from care
Free from all earthly sin
Open wide the door of love
And let such people in.

Notes

GARRY SAYS:

Two little boys went fishing
Into the sea of nod.
In the cutest little boat,
With the cutest little rod.
And tho' I don't believe it
I have heard them say,
That they caught all the big fish,
That from Daddy got away.
They say the boat was loaded
'Til it could hold no more,
So they shook out the sails again,
And headed for the shore.
But something must have happened,
For they got a surprise,
When they wakened in the morning
And opened up their eyes.
They really looked quite mystified,
But after all they said;
We really were out fishing
Although we' er still in bed.

Notes

GET READY NOW

Don't wait too long, 'til its too late.
Don't let this Empire share the fate,
Of Holland, Poland, Belgium, France,
Get ready now for now's our chance.
Get ready now let us defy,
On land and sea and in the sky,
The challenge of the cursed Huns.
Let us reply with blazing guns.
Think-think well of all those lands
Now crushed beneath the ruthless hands
Of him who would be king of all.
Let us finish him, against a wall.
We who each night get safe to bed,
No enemy bombing raids to dread.
We think it cannot happen here
We're far away and do not fear,
Yes, get ready now and lets make sure
Lets show the Huns their bad mistake
For the British Empire they'll never Break.

Notes

GLENN SAYS:

I like to imagine my bed is a boat
And often to wonderful sea's I will float
I am the captain and Garry the crew
And oh, but the wonderful things that we do.
We go searching for treasure,
For jewels and gold
Hidden for years by the pirate's of old.
We sail faery rivers to out of way places
And once met some people
with the cutest black faces.
We once paid a call to a cannabal isle
And stayed with the king and the queen for a while.
T'was really a wonderful time that we had,
And leaving the place made me feel quite sad.
And so as our sails fill out with the breeze

Onward we sail through these beautiful sea's
'Til at last we drop anchor in old sleepy bay,
Then I shut my eyes tight until sleep comes my way.

Notes

HERO

I remember seeing Daddy, kissing Mum good-by,
And saying, oh so gently, cheer up do not cry.
And then he turned to me and said
"Son your quite a man,
You look after Mummy always, help her all you can."
My throat got sort of lumpy, I tried to force a smile.
And said, "But, Daddy,
you'll be back in just a little while.
Then this war will be over and you'll put away
your gun,
And we'll all be together, and boy, won't we have fun."
Then we can go out fishing, Dad, like you said we'd do.
Tho' women do not like to fish, we'll take Mummy too.
In summer-time we'll go and camp,
like Indians on the plain.
Everything will sure be swell
when you come home again."
But yesterday a letter came as letters sometimes do.
It said that Dad had disappeared up in the sky so blue.
I remembered what he said to me and so I didn't cry.
That isn't tears your seeing now
-it's some thing in my eye.

But I will keep my promise, Dad, I'll look after Mum.
And in my heart you'll always be a hero and a chum.
And when I do go fishing, you'll be there just the same.
For Mummy says you havn't gone, we'll meet
somewhere again..

HILLS O' HAME

I'd like to now it's summer
Go sailing up the Clyde
An' visit back in Scotland
Where my thoughts still bide.
I'd like to visit Glasgow toon
An' hear auld Reekie's story
An' climb the heights tae Arthurs's seat
An' view the ancient glory
Once more to see the heather bloom
The burnies singin' as they run
An' see the moon come ower the ben
At even' when the day is done.
Once more to hear the cuckoo call
The larks gay song at early morn.
An' mist enshrouded hills emerge
Tae beauty as the day is born.
Land o' Wallace, Bruce an' Burns,
O' Scott and bold Rob Roy,
Land o' mountains, lochs and glens
I wandered as a boy.
Sweet the thoughts that `round you linger,
Ah, the magic o' yer name
An' I'd like to, now it's summer
See once mair, the hills o' hame.

Notes

HOPE

I was talking to the spirit of Edgar Allen Poe,
And he told me of his troubles
when he tried to get a show.
He looked at me quite kindly, smiled, and then he said,
"Cheer up, Allan Matthews,
you'll be famous when you're dead."
When you climb the golden stairway,
And St. Peter's hand you've wrung,
Then the plaudits of the people shall at
your feet be flung.
They'll appreciate your efforts,
and then they will, I trust,
Erect to you a statue, or a little marble bust."
Through life, my friend, you'll always strive,
but fate is ever fickle.
Your appetite she'll always whet,
your palate never tickle.
A gift you have, some people think,
the gifts of thoughts to pen,
Ability to read the dreams, the minds,
and hearts of men.
The fates have cast you in a role,
you must play to the end.

Your road is long, for hope you'll search,
`round every turn and bend.
But let your heart have courage,
and remember as you go.
That your struggle, was the struggle,
of Edgar Allen Poe.

I REMEMBER

I remember Hell-fire
Corner and those wild days of '18
When we were writing "Finis"
To a madman's war machine.

I remember the Meuse and Y'pres
And the battles of the Somme
Where so many hero's died
On fields so far from home.

I remember, yes, so clearly,
As time me memories bridge,
To where Canada made history
On the slopes of Vimy Ridge.

I remember too, my comrades
who died before they'd yield
Who lie amidst the poppies
In far off Flanders Fields.

All these things I remember
As with uncovered head
I stand before the Cenotaph
Paying homage to the dead.

Notes

IN RETROSPECT

A dreaming hour, a backward thought That flows
And like a summer flower That grows
Within the garden of memory a while Shall bring
a smile.
Perhaps a tear, a petal small Shall fall
But still the thought in friendship wrought Shall be
A kindly and a treasured memory.

Notes

INDEPENDENCE

To reach the state of independence
Is the goal of every man.
To be a gentleman of leisure.
Is a universal plan.
No more Monday mornings,
When your feeling, not just right,
After you have whooped it up
Sat.and Sunday night.
No more punching time clocks,
Or watching for the boss.
Wondering what the hell you'd do,
In case your job you lost.
No more money headaches,
Or a dull sense of defeat,
Feeling that your in a rut,
Up a dead end street.
No more this and no more that,
The sun upon you beams
But me my friend, I reach it, yes.
When I'm in bed in dreams.

Notes

INTERNATIONAL INCIDENT

(Used in a recent news report)

Frae lip tae lip the news went round,
The Scots were good an' mad.
A Yankee chiel, had tried tae steal
The Royal Stewart plaid.

The fiery cross went ower the hill,
A war was almost startin',
Nae alien hips must bear a kilt
o' brave Prince Charley's tartan.

The warpipes o' the Scottish clans
Were heard in awsome skirlin'
An' rumbles echoed o'er the land
Like thunder over Stirlin'.

But ere the pikes were oot the thatch,
The Scots sere a' disbandin',
Frae ower the water came the word
Twas a' misunderstandin'.

Lack o' knowledge caused the stir,
The Scottish race tae shuggle,
Aye, just a lack o' tartan lore
He thought it was MacDougall!

Notes

હ

JIM…

I knew him as a boy so long ago,
We never thought -but then how could we know?
The horrors that this world would in store,
And he'd lie dead, a soldier, on a foreign shore.

Together, we had often gone to school,
He loved to play, to fight, or just to fool,
A brother, aye, far dearer than a friend,
I bet he was a soldier to the end.

Notes

JUST FISHIN'

Nothing like a shady stream
Where a man can sit and dream
Just fishin'.

Sure a pleasure, mighty fine,
With his back against a pine.
Sittin' there with rod an' line
Just fishin'.

Listenin' to the waters play,
Seems to ease his cares away.
Brightens up a fellers day,
Just fishin'

Yep! A man feels more content
By an idle hour that's spent
Just fishin'.

Notes

LIKE A ROCK

Standing as she's stood for ages,
A little island in the sea.
She has wrote in history's pages,
Deeds for all eternity.

Famed she is in song and story,
Fighting in the cause of right.
Seeking not a winners glory,
Keeping freedoms torch alight.

Like a beacon brightly burning,
Stronger growing day by day.
From her goal there is no turning, '
til she's crushed oppressions way.

Standing as she's stood for ages,
With truth and freedom, hand in hand,
It shall be wrote in history's pages
Still unconquered, England stands.

Notes

LUDWIG

Ludwig was a soldier in the Africander Korp,
And he dreamed of shooting Englishmen
and Yankees by the score,
So they gave Lud a Mauser, and a suit of
German green,
And sent him off to Africa for him to vent his spleen.
Now Ludwig thought the Germans were a super
duper race,
And Englishmen, just Englishmen, with a senile
kind of face.
So Ludwig's heart beat proudly as he marched
behind Rommel,
Up the valley of the Nile to give the Allies hell.
When Ludwig woke that morning – it was by the
powder smell,
He murmured 'Donnerwetter' I'm dead and gone
to hell."
But with courage that's a product of his super duper race
He scrambled bravely to his feet and showed the
Wops his pace.

The sand was hot and deep and loose, and Lud
began to tire,
His tongue was out quite hard and parched,
his innards were on fire
The sun shone down its molten heat from out the
brassy sky
But Lud says " It's for Germany and gave another try.
He gave a spurt, his legs they flashed,
the sands they fairly churned.
The Wops he passed at awful speed,
the track he surely burned.
And when he led the pack at last,
a smile lit up his face,
"The Wops," he snorted "can't outrun
the super-duper race.
He dug a trench and bedded down like
others of his kind,
While Rommel watched the enemy,
their weakest spot to find.
But Monty was a foxy guy, who played up to a hunch,
And right into
the Germans' pants he shot his Sunday punch.

MACKILT'S CONFESSION

Its rare commando training
I indulge in every night.
The survival of the fittest
Is the battle that I fight.

I've got some copper sheathing
That I wear beneath my coat
And I can prance and butt around
Like old MacGinty's goat.

I wear around my ankles too
Some socks of processed steel.
And I ignore the batterings
Of spike and Cuban heel.

I'm almost as well armored
As a medium Whippet tank
What do I care if people stare
Or wonder at the clank.

I really like to travel now
Unlike the days of yore.
When gasping, breathless, I was crushed
Or tramped upon the floor.

I'm a well protected fellow, folks.
No more I mind the fuss,
Of travelling by street car. Yes.
Or even in a bus.

MEMORIES

Light as fancy thoughts go flying
Backward down the years,
Bringing reminiscent smiles,
Sometimes, too, the tears,
Memories – like rays of sunlight
Stored against the cold,
Cheer us in our lonely moments,
When we're worn and old.

Notes

MEMORIES OF CHILDHOOD

How sweet are the memories of childhood we treasure
As backward our thoughts to our infancy run.
The friendships we knew still bring us some pleasure
Though vanished, like mist in the new risen sun.

How quickly the days of our childhood are over,
And into the turmoil of life we are thrust.
How often, in dreaming, our thoughts again hover
On plans that we cherished, now turned into dust..
Age may o'ertake us; the years in Their passing
May bend us a little, like wind-driven grain,
But a word, or a name,
and thoughts will come massing,
To make vivid the scenes of our childhood again.
Oh, Lord, stretch out thy Hand and bless
All sinners such as me For only you the power possess
To set all people free

Notes

OH LORD

Oh, Lord, stretch out thy Hand and bless
All sinners such as me
For only you the power possess
To set all people free

Notes

ON ST. ANDREW'S DAY

Like old Rabbie, I'm no gifted,
And I'm no a Walter Scott,
And I canna pen the pictures
Often borne to me in thought.
Craggy hills and rugged mountains
Climbing upward to the sky,
Come to me in vision often,
As my thoughts in fancy fly.
Once again I see Loch Lomond
Sparkle 'neath the summer sun,
And the even' shadows gather
Round the hens when day is done.
Sweetly comes the scent o' heather
Mingled wi' the tang o' pine,
And I give a sigh, half longing,
For the days o' auld lang syne.

Notes

PIXIE PETE

I've lost my way, cried Pixie Pete,
I just don't understand,
In what direction I have come,
Or where is fairy-land.
An old crow croaked down from his tree,
You're in a fix, my lad.
Boys that wander far from home,
I think are really bad.
The wise old owl then shook his head,
As solemn as can be,
Tut, tut, he muttered in his beard,
How bad those youngsters be.
But Sammy Sparrow heard the cry,
And pausing in his flight, He said,
don't cry my little friend,
I know the way all right.
So Pixie Pete got home again,
Now him you rarely see,
For he has promised to be good,
As good, as good, can be.

Notes

PRAYER

God give him sight that he may see again,
The beauties thou hast wrought upon this land.
The blessedness of light to him restore,
By the gracious magnanimity of thy hand.

Notes

REMEMBERING

I remember the feeling at Christmas
When I, just a slip of a lad,
Hung up my stocking on Christmas Eve,
Ah, the glorious dreams that I had.
Before I would climb into bed,
I'd take one last look at the sky
Hoping that Santa would sure find our house,
Just hoping he wouldn't pass by.
And long before sleep came my way,
I'd listen, as if for some proof Perhaps
for the jingle of bells,
Or the sound of a sleigh on the roof I know that the
children today,
Have the dreams that I had as a boy.
And I hope that old Santa will find every house
So they too may look back and enjoy The thrill as you
hang up your stocking
With a heart that is youthful and gay
Yes, the thrill as you hang up your stocking
On the Eve of a bright Christmas Day.

Notes

REVERIE

Autumn leaves, in crimson, gold, and brown
With each light breeze to earth come tumbling down.
And naked trees stand stark in field and dell
And silently of passing Seasons tell.
The Summer's gone, and soon
King Winter's hand Shall spread his mantle white,
Across the land.
And from his throne, with icy breath,
He'll reign, Until the joyous Spring
Shall come again.

Notes

SCOTLAND'S AWAKE

There's no need to worry, Scotland's awake
If Hitler takes England he'll find his mistake;
If he crosses the border, his story he'll tell
To the rest of his kind if they accept him in hell.
I just can't imagine those sons of the heather
Giving in to old Adolf or showing the white feather.
If they land up in Scotland it'll go tough with Fritz,
For they're all set to give them a little Scotch Blitz.
They'll whittle them down like a field full of Barley
Will the sons of the sons who followed Prince Charley
So there's no need to worry, just ease your mind,
There'll always be an England, Scotland's behind.

Notes

SLOW DOWN TO FORTY

He looked like a thrifty old Scotchman
All dressed in his bonnet and kilt.
And there he sat there in the picture
On the cheapest wee car ever built.
In fancy we could hear him chuckle
Explaining to us with a smile.
"It canna dae forty or fifty,
But laddies I'm settin the style.
Speedin' is nae patriotic
To ken it's a wastage o' gas
Noo my car is real economic
Its cheapness you canna surpass
It doesn't need gassin' or oilin'
An' tho' maybe it makes me perspire
I'm savin' now too on the rubber
Just look at the size o' the tire
Remember this time we'er all fighting
And tighten your belt up a notch
To practice a little economy
Just take a tip frae us Scotch.
Yes, He looked like a thrifty old Scotchman
His advice you'll admit was quite sound
By keeping your speed under forty
You'll be keeping our planes off the ground.

Notes

SONG AT TWILIGHT

When the sun goes down beyond the hill,
Ere twilight deepens into night,
Or from their haven in the -sky,
stars begin to shed their light
From some dusk-shrouded glen there comes,
In accents rising dear and shrill,
As if to bid the day farewell,
The falling of the Whippoorwill.

Notes

SUNDOWN FROM THE HILL

The sun in crimson splendor, In the west,
Was sinking slowly, labor o'er, And to rest.
When in the hush of evening Calm and still,
I slowly walked the pathway, On the hill.
Below – the river runs on to the sea,
Its whisper muted As if in reverie.
And far beyond, the hills, In hazy blue,
Take on the garb of night's More solemn hue.
The day is done. The sun No more remains aloof,
But lightly fingers, ere she goes, Each roof,
As if some hope and courage to impart,
Deep down within the confines of each heart.

Notes

SURVIVAL OF THE FITTEST

It's rare commando training I indulge in every night.
The survival of the fittest Is the battle that I fight.
I've got some copper sheathing
That I wear beneath my coat,
And I can prance and butt around
Like old MacGinty's goat.
I wear around my ankles, too,
Some socks of processed steel,
And I ignore the batterings
Of spike and Cuban heel.
I'm almost as well armoured
As a medium Whippet tank.
What do I care if people stare
Or wonder at the clank.
I really like to travel now,
Unlike the days of yore.
When gasping, breathless,
I was crushed
Or tramped upon the floor.
I'm a well protected fellow, folks,
No more I mind the fuss,
Of travelling by street-car.
Yes, Or even in a bus.

Notes

THAT I MAY SEE THY LIGHT

Help me, guide me
Down the path
Of ___, of right
Lead me, teach me
By thy word
That I may see thy light.

Notes

THE AFTER-CHRISTMAS TREE
FORGOTTEN

In the snow it lies
Its glitter gone.
But still there clings
As if by careless hands Left,
Here and there,
A tinselled icicle.
A tiny memory
Which seems to say.
Of how it stood, Awhile,
King for a day.

Notes

THE BAGPIPES

Despite all this cussin' and fussin'
as to whether the bagpipes are musical
instruments or not,
to the Scot they will always be
Pipes of war and pipes of glory,
Pipes that thrill the Scottish heart.
Pipes renowned in song and story,
That of Scotland is a part.
Pipes that sing of misty moorlands,
Hills of heath and heather braes.
Pipes that tell of shady valleys
Heaven in their winding ways.
Pipes that sing of faith and courage
Gallant hearts and hope reborn.
Pipes that tell of foemen vanquished
Like the mist before the morn.
Pipes that tell an ancient story
Bringing visions to the eye
Kilted clansmen gaily marching
Somewhere `neath a foreign sky. . .
Maybe I'm just optimistic?
But when mankind reach the moon,
A kilted lad -with highland bagpipes
Leads them forth with highland tune.

Notes

THE COMMON FIGHTING MAN

Let Generals and Admirals Gather glory as they can.
The backbone of the nation
Is her common fighting man.
The gallant old foot-slogger
With his bayonet and his gun
Is the man who'll do the fighting
Ere our final victory's won.
He's the heart of every army,
The core of every plan;
He's the backbone of the nation,
Is the common fighting man.
He's only Private Someone,
He may be low in rank, But after this is over
It's him we'll have to thank.
He'll keep our Empire's glory safe
From Hun or yellow man;
So let us give the credit due
The common fighting man.

Notes

THE DODO BIRDS

I've often heard the dodo bird
Was lazy, tired, and slow,
And passed away, some people say,
Three hundred years ago.

Records state this birdie's fate
Was due to one condition.
It wouldn't work, preferred to shirk,
It just had no ambition.

And then there's folk, who love a joke,
Who tell me with some grousing
These birds ain't dead, but are instead,
Behind this war-time housing.

Notes

THE EMPIRE

From India to Africa our battle flags unfurled
And backward ever backward the enemy is hurled
From the Burma Road to Tripoli they'll hear
our victory cry
And with it dinning in their ears the enemy will die.

Notes

WHO

Who bandaged your little cut fingers,
    Kissing away all your tears?
Who crooned you to sleep every bedtime,
    Soothing away all your fears?
Who is that wonderful lady,
    Through lifetime we all think divine?
That wonderful lady – your mother –
    Just your mother and mine.

Notes

THE GALLANT 51ST

Can't you vision, clear, the desert,
a hot and burning sun,
A dust cloud moving quickly,
as the foemen break and run,
Can't you hear, though just in fancy,
a sound that greets your ear?
Some voices raised in shouting, aye,
a lusty Scottish cheer.

Can't you see the mighty battle like
a waters ebb and flow,
Or hear the thunder `o the guns or
a bayonets thudding blow.
Can't you see where it's the thickest,
where hell on earths the worst.
These gallant men from hill and glen,
old Scotland's fifty-first.

Can't you hear the pibroch skirlin',
its grand old victory cry?
Can't you see the foemen huddled,
as trembling they die.

Can't you see the bonnie Gordons and the
lads from old Argyle,
Marching forward wi' the Camerons, their faces
wreathed in smiles?
Can't you see the gallant Seaforths reeve in their belts
a notch,
And step it out through burning sand along
with the Black Watch?
It sets your heart to stirring and you almost
burst wi' pride,
How could we lose in any fight wi' such men
on our side?
Fresh honors to old Scotland they have brought thro'
blood and sweat.
Through Scottish courage like this shown,
the Axis sun shall set.
Let all Dictators rave and rant,
bring on you fiends your worst.
I'll drink a toast to Scotland yet and her gallant 51st.

THE HOOK AND LADDER CREW

"My father is a fireman," said Kenny with a grin.
He's a jolly old smoke-eater,
who'll fight thro' thick and thin.
He's the cheeriest of laddies that ever flushed a flue.
And the sturdiest wee member of the hook and
ladder crew.

He's never really happy 'til of smoke he's got the smell
And his truck is out and rollin' with a clangin'
o' the bell.
He's right in there a-pitchin' and he'll stay
and see it through.
With the other rugged members of the hook
and ladder crew.

When smoke goes up in volume like a pillar to the sky
You can tell he's really happy by the twinkle in his eye
Tho' the waters cold an' freezin'
an' his face and hands are blue.
He'll fight for that's the spirit of the hook
and ladder crew.

They never spare the motor as they race on
down the street
And they're muffled up in oilskins from their head down
to their feet,
They can smell a fire further than Adolf can a Jew
They're mighty gallant fellows on the hook
and ladder crew.

THE MISTY YEARS

When the years roll by and we're worn and old
And the flame of youth is gone,
When our dreams are dust and hope no more
Is a staff to lean upon,
Then we'll give a sigh, a wistful sigh,
For the days that used to be,
And we'll drift back down the misty years
To live with a memory.

Notes

THE MOON

If the impossible could happen
If the moon could only write
Of the scenes that she has witnessed
On her travels thro' the night.
If our old moon could only talk
What a story she'd unfold
For all that she has seen and heard
Would make the greatest story told
From this worlds beginning
From the very mists of time
She has gazed upon mans folly
In every land and clime.
She has seen man in his happiness
Such as only love can yield.
She has gazed on death and sorrow
On every battle field.
She has seen vast empires flourish
From nations that were small.
She has seen them in their glory.
She has seen them rot and fall.

She has seen a million wonders
On her trips across the sky
Up there so many miles away
A calm all-seeing eye.
If she could only stop and write
Her story some day soon
It would be well worth reading
"My Memories" by the Moon.

THE TORCH

The torch of freedom you must keep,
Against oppression, burning.
Keep the faith with us who sleep,
By from your path not turning.
We too suffered, bled and died,
We, too, knew war, and horror.
Our heart's like yours, for rest had cried,
And dreaded the to-morrow.
Keep the torch of freedom lit,
For it we gladly died.
Until that time when men again,
On earth, in peace, abide.

Notes

THE WINNER

We have shuddered at its passing,
At its frigid icy breath,
That Reaper, grim, that scavenger,
That shadows us called death.
How awful the futility,
You can't escape his noose.
No dodging or agility,
Can beat him on the loose.
We're born a sure fatality,
He gets us in the end.
No hope of immortality,
Awaits us round the bend.
His step has never wavered,
He has always been the same,
A scavenger, ill-favored,
But the winner in the game.

Notes

A GRAY HAIRED LADY

Theres a gray haired lady sitting
An' she's busy wi' her knitting
But her thought are wi' her son
    Across the sea.

An' she'll sometimes gi' a sigh
For a day that's long gone by.
When he was but a lad
    Upon her knee.

A tear may gather in her eye
Life canna be the same.
So she sits there knitting, waiting,
For that laddie tae come hame.

Notes

THEY WERE MEN

Will the story be told in the years that's to come
Of the fight in that desert of sand.
Will the story be told of the deeds that were done
In that heat ridden hell of a land.

Will we read of the men, who, after retreat,
Held the line solid and fast.
Men in whose hearts was no thought of defeat
No enemy ever yet passed.

Will we read of their trek 'neath the hot searing sun
As they moved up the line in full kit.
Will we know of their daring while routing the Hun,
These hero's just "doing their bit".
What were the thoughts the dreams or the hopes
Of the sons of the Empire who fell.
Does the wind carry back to some sandy slope
The sound of a sweet victory bell.
Who would attempt it, for what author could
Write such a saga with pen,
But they'll get the credit as they surely should
For they've proven, by gad, they were men.

Notes

THOUGHTS

Each night when I get lonely
Wherever I may be
My thoughts reach backward through the years
And once again I see

A sheiling on the hillside
Where the purple heather grows.
Its memory lingers sweetly
As the evening shadows close.

Back there my heart goes longing,
And its there that I would be
For that sheiling on the hillside
Is ever home to me.

Notes

TO GAIL

As through the sea's of life you sail
We hope good fortune shall prevail.
And all your dreams what'ere they are
Shall blossom 'neath a lucky star.

We hope your skies are always blue
In troubles lass come smiling thro'.
We hope your luck shall never fail,
Oh, little fair haired girlie, Gail.

Notes

TO HITCH

Congratulations, dash it all.
From us fellows great and small
We wish you luck beyond compare
With this your brand new son and heir.

You've entered a new phase of life
A strenous time of man and wife.
But stick it out thro' thick and thin,
This era of the safety pin.

He'll be a joy to Uncles, Aunts
This laddie in three cornered pants.
You'll have your fun, I have no doubt.
But "hitch" melad, your works cut out.

From now on it's "Jack my dear"'
The time for feeding baby's near.
Its Jack do this or Jack do that
You'll wonder where the heck you're at.

But work like this is always fun ??????
And after all it must be done.
Remember as we shake your fins,
You can thank your stars it wasn't twins.

Notes

TO SID

On that far day that Adam,
Found it thrilling squeezing Eve,
He invented a great pastime,
Quite the greatest, I believe.
It has come down the ages,
As no other pastime did,
And now it's reached the Lower Lab.
And made a mess of Sid.
In fact he likes this game so much
This cuddle, kiss, and squeeze,
He's going to get hitched to the girl,
And do it at his ease
We have tried to stop his folly,
With advice of every kind.
Even shown him scars of battle,
But to all, our Sidney's blind.
He has bitten at the apple
And he treats our words with scorn.
He has savoured of this pastime,
That was with Adam born.

We have tried to pierce his armour,
To find some vital spark
But Sid will only see the light
Long after it's too dark
The wisdom of us veterans
Has fallen by the way,
Killed by the gleam in Sidney's eyes,
"Der Tag" it seems to say.
And so we quit, discouraged,
But still we'll give a thought,
Upon the day the preacher,
Tie's poor Sidney in a knot.

TO SUPERMAN

As I lay dreaming dreams one night,
A vision came to me.
I saw a man, a super-man,
Who said his name was Lee.

I heard his smooth voice flowing on,
His words so like a Sage's.
He said he'd solved the mystery of,
All women's moods and ages.

I heard my own voice cry aloud,
"No man yet lives who can,
Plum the depth as deep as that
Not even Super-man.

He answered, "Yes, by psychic force,
I've solved what puzzled Adam,
No woman now can puzzle me,
Be she Miss or Madam. . . "

O was the Lord the giftie gie us,
Tai see ourselves as others see us,
To see ourselves throught other eyes
Would gie most folks a great suprise.

Notes

TO YOU – FROM ME

Noo ma uncle an' ma faither,
They went flyin' o'er the sea.
Back tae Bonnie Scotland
Just like folk o' high degree.
They had guid times wi' MacKenzie,
An' the Campbells – a' the lot.
Why michty me, a day ne'er passed
They were'na both half shot...

And there it must end, for the brain is
as empty tonight as a
Scotsman's purse on flag day. However,
to you who will read
the enclosed verses I would like to say. . .

I seek no fortune, have no claim
These words will find undying fame.
Just give the thought "at least he tried"
And I, my friend, am satisfied.

Notes

VISION

Can you see the big tanks rolling,
O'er the deserts ancient sands
As steadily they march on, mile by mile?
Can you hear the big guns thunder,
Manned by eager willing hands
Of the valiant British Army of the Nile?

Can you hear the airplanes spitting,
Dealing death from out the sky,
As forward, ever forward, goes the thrust?
Can you see the foeman vanquished
His hopes of conquest gone
As his armies fall to mingle with the dust?

Can you see the men in khaki
Sweeping onward like a flood,
Their sweating, grimy faces in a smile?
Do you thank God for England
And the Allies who are there
With the valiant British Army of the Nile?

Notes

WAITING FOR SPRING

The frigid hand of winter grips
Each valley, dale, and hill.
And silent now the music of Each woodl
and stream and rill.
Behind yon barn the cattle stand
In shelter from the blast,
And silently perhaps they dream
Of summer days gone past.
Or then again, perhaps like me,
Though winter winds still sing,
They wait a bit impatiently
The coming of the Spring.

Notes

WE CANNOT CEASE

The guns of war re-echo o'er the world
Against the common foe our might is hurled
On land and sea and above us in the sky
We're fighting that our freedom shall not die.

The lords of hate who over us would rule
Must perish ere our cause is won
And tho' we know the blood, the sweat and tears
We cannot cease until the work is done.

Notes

WHAT ANSWER HAVE YOU?

War is a cruel dreadful thing.
Just the word itself has a cruel ring.
It conjures up visions of thundering guns,
Of fighting fathers, husbands, sons.
Of cities blasted from the air,
Cities that once were proud and fair.
Of boats torpedoed far at sea.
Ah, God! How cruel war can be.
Nights of horror, homes aflame,
And one man only for this to blame.
But a day of reckoning there soon shall be
When those that are like him as well as he
Are called to atone for this awful sin.
What answer have you, you beast of Berlin?
'Thou Shalt Not Kill' are the words of our Lord.
What answer have you for drawing the sword?

Notes

WHO

Who bandaged your little cut fingers,
Kissing away all your tears?
Who crooned you to sleep every bedtime,
Soothing away all your fears?
Who is that wonderful lady,
Through lifetime we all think divine?
That wonderful lady -your mother
Just your mother and mine.

Notes

WISHES UNFULFILED

Sorta wishin' for the summer,
Kinda tired of cold an' snow.
Sorta waitin' for the springtime
And the grass again to grow.

Sorta tired of sweepin' sidewalks,
Splittin' wood an' heavin' coal.
Diggin' out from under snowdrifts
Makes me feel just like a mole.

Sorta hankerin' for breezes
That don't freeze you to the bone.
Sorta tired of zero weather
Chillin' hands an' feet to stone.

Sorta tired of heavy clothin',
And goloshes on my feet.
Kinda hate this slippy walkin'
When I'm strollin' down the street.

Sorta wishin' for the springtime,
Friendly suns an' smilin' skies
Poison ivy, ants, mosquitoes,
Spiders, bugs, and bloomin' flies.

Notes

THIS COUNTRY OF MINE

The Irish may sing of Killarney
And the valleys and dells of Kildare.
And tell, with a gay touch of blarney,
Of Erin so lovely and fair.

The Scotsman may sing of Loch Lomond,
And the bloom on the bonnie bluebell.
And be loud in his praise of the heathery braes
And of mountain, of woodland and dell.

The English may sigh of Old England
And the beauties of England in Spring
Of the bloom on the rose, and how lovely it grows
His voice will in ecstasy ring. . .

But give me the land where the Rockies
Raise pinnacled peaks to the sky
So proud and aloof and majestic
Where echoes the wild eagle's cry.

Give me the land of the maple
The spruce and the evergreen pine
No country, in beauty, can ever
Compare with this country of mine.

Notes

CANADA

Have we no poet to sing about
The glories of this land?
To sit awhile, and dream awhile,
And then with pen in hand
To write in deep undying words
The glory of her mountains,
And sing of how the summer sun
Goes sparkling from her fountains?
From where, like tow'ring battlements,
The Rockies proudly soar
To where the blue Pacific in triumph
Sweeps the shore,
By prairie, plain and river,
Kind nature's lavish hand
Has sprinkled deep with beauty
Each corner of this land.
Have we no poet, by such inspired,
To wield a fluent pen,
And bring the beauties of this land
Close to the hearts of men?
For where's the country, where's the place,
What far off foreign strand,
Can e' er compare in beauty to The beauty of this land?